D0116872

RODEO DAY

by JoNelle Toriseva
illustrated by Robert Casilla

BRADBURY PRESS NEW YORK

Maxwell Macmillan Canada Toronto
Maxwell Macmillan International
New York Oxford Singapore Sydney

Bradbury Press
Macmillan Publishing Company
866 Third Avenue
New York, NY 10022

Maxwell Macmillan Canada, Inc.
1200 Eglinton Avenue East
Suite 200
Don Mills, Ontario M3C 3N1

Macmillan Publishing Company is part of the Maxwell Communication Group of Companies.

The text of this book is set in Aster.
The art is rendered in watercolor on illustration board with some use of pastel and colored pencils.

First edition
Printed and bound in Hong Kong by South China Printing Company (1988) Ltd.
10 9 8 7 6 5 4 3 2 1

LIBRARY OF CONGRESS CATALOGING-IN-PUBLICATION DATA
Toriseva, JoNelle.
Rodeo Day / by JoNelle Toriseva ; illustrated by Robert Casilla.—1st ed.
p. cm.
Summary: After years of traveling around the state watching the bigger kids compete, Lacey experiences the thrill of riding in her first rodeo.
ISBN 0-02-789405-3
[1. Rodeos—Fiction.] I. Casilla, Robert, ill. II. Title.
PZ7.T6445Ro 1994
[E]—dc20 92-39475

ACKNOWLEDGMENTS: The author wishes to thank members of the National High School Rodeo Association, the Minnesota High School Rodeo Association, the Little Britches Rodeo Association, and Jim Chanley. The artist extends appreciation to models Emily Egginton, Colleen Gilbert, and Christine Gilbert, and everyone at West Orchard Elementary School, Chappaqua, New York, especially librarian Carolyn Cagle.

To my two rodeoing sisters,
Julia and Jerianne

—J.T.

To my little cowboy,
Robert, Jr.

—R.C.

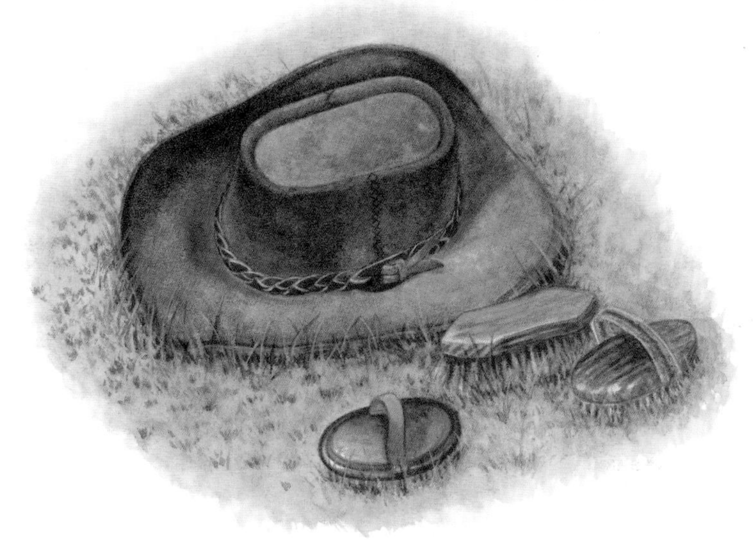

Sweet Gussie smells of clover and alfalfa. Lacey leans against her strong flank and breathes deeply. For years Lacey has traveled to rodeos around the state, watching her older sister Julia compete. Starting today, she's not just a helper or a watcher anymore. Today she will ride in her first rodeo.

Lacey braids a tiny section down the center of Gussie's tail and ties it at the bottom with a red ribbon. Then she stands on the steel water pail and ties a smaller bow at the top of Gussie's rump. Gussie's ribbons match the ones in Lacey's French braid.

Lacey climbs into the camper.

She turns around and around, worrying. *What if my jeans rip? What if I make a mistake?*

There isn't enough room to hide in a pickup camper.

There's a knock. "Are you in there? I've got a present for you."

"Katie! You're here."

Katie Wolf climbs in. Katie is Lacey's best friend in the rodeo. Even though they live 259 miles apart, they see each other almost every weekend during the spring and fall at rodeos around the state.

"Happy first rodeo!" Katie says, and hands her a box wrapped in blue.

Lacey opens the package and holds up a blue-and-white western-yoked shirt. "It's beautiful!"

"Mom made it for you to wear today," Katie says. "For good luck."

Lacey says, "All those people coming to see the rodeo are going to be in the stands by two o'clock."

"It's fun, Lacey. They'll see you in your new shirt."

"I used to like looking at their faces and seeing all the little kids jump up and down. I liked all the clapping and yelling. But today..."

"Today you'll be *in* the rodeo. That's the only difference. Everything else is the same."

"Today people can see me."

Katie hugs her. "Hey, everybody gets nervous. But you'll do great."

"Thanks for the shirt," Lacey says.

Katie leaves to go get ready.

Lacey and Julia have a lot to do, too. Without talking, they brush Gussie until her honey brown coat shines. Julia throws Dad's old blue saddle pad over one side of Gussie, and Lacey catches it on the other. Then Julia lifts the heavy saddle on. Lacey pulls the stirrup down on her side.

After they've saddled Sweet Gussie, Lacey practices hitching her to the side of the trailer. Each time Lacey keeps her hands smooth as she knots the reins as fast as she can. Gussie swats flies with her tail, ignoring Lacey.

“Look at this,” says Julia. “Here are our names on the program.”

“Where’s mine?”

“You’re number five, right under Little Britches Junior Girls’ Goat-tail Tying. See?”

“Where are you?” Lacey asks.

“Look under High School Rodeo Girls’ Goat-tying.”

“Julia Johnson! We’re famous.”

“Very famous,” Julia says.

Sweet Gussie swings her head toward them and neighs softly. Lacey walks over and puts her arms around Gussie's big neck. Gussie whinnies.

"There are things to be scared about," Lacey says to her. Gussie nuzzles against Lacey. She has been a rodeo horse for a long time.

From the cooler sitting under the trailer, Lacey grabs a stalk of celery. Gussie shakes her head when she sees the treat. Lacey loves to hear her chomp, chomp, chomp.

"Scared?" asks Julia as she sits down on the wheel hub of the trailer.

"I'm afraid I'll fall off. There's so much to remember...."

"You've practiced so much, you could do it underwater upside down," Julia says, and buckles on her belt with the large silver buckle she won last year at the Snake River Roundup Rodeo.

"I wish I could be in goat tying, like you. Not just tail tying," Lacey says.

"When you're fourteen, then you get to do it."

"If they'd let me do it now, I could help Dad catch and cure the sick calves, like you get to do."

"You're learning, Lacey. Today you'll prove it."

Julia mounts Sweet Gussie. Lacey hops up to sit behind the saddle. To warm Gussie up, they walk around the back of the arena. Then they trot in the field behind the rows of horse trailers, campers, pickups, and tents. Along with the other rodeo families, they have made an instant neighborhood-on-wheels.

Dad walks beside them as they ride Sweet Gussie to the arena. They line up with the other kids.

Everyone in the rodeo rides in the grand entry. Lacey yelps as they race into the arena close to the front-runner. They weave in and out in a snake pattern behind the U.S. flag, the state flag, and the rodeo banners. The banners crack in the wind. The horses kick up the dirt in the arena. The dirt smells of cows, and the arena is the same oval Lacey practiced in. With the people in the stands, though, everything is different.

As "The Star-Spangled Banner" begins, they race out. Katie gallops by and waves as the events begin.

First, the bucking bulls: Black Magic, Chili Pepper, Steam Roller, and Dynamite Dill Pickle throw their riders. The clowns roll away from the hooves of the bucking horses. The cowgirls race around the barrels. The riders each rope a calf, and finally it is time for the goat-tail tying event.

17

Sweet Gussie and Lacey walk through the gate. They stand alone in the arena. Hundreds of people watch from the bleachers. Lacey pushes her cowboy hat down further on her head. The hot dogs and beans Dad cooked for lunch twist in her stomach.

Lacey stares at the goat one hundred yards ahead. She stares only at it. To prepare herself to start the clock, Lacey cuts Gussie into a sharp turn and stands up in the stirrups. Then they race past the signal. The seconds start ticking.

Lacey kicks Sweet Gussie's flanks. They gallop across the starting line. People yell, but Lacey can't hear the words. Her hat falls off. When they are near the goat, Lacey swings her right leg over the saddle to make a flying dismount. For a moment her left heel catches in the stirrup.

Before she loses her balance, Lacey kicks out her heel. Gussie slides to a stop. Lacey touches the dirt running and ties her to the hitch. Then she runs toward the goat.

Lacey reaches out to grab the goat, and it runs away. She runs and catches it. Lacey holds the goat between her legs and ties the ribbon on the short, scraggly tail. Her hands shake.

To show she's finished her tie, Lacey throws her hands into the air. It's not over yet. If Gussie comes off the hitch or the ribbon unties or if it has taken her over a minute to do all this, Lacey will be disqualified. The five seconds go on and on. A bull bellows near the corral. The cows stamp in back of the stock trucks. The crowd whirls around the arena. Lacey tastes dirt on her teeth. She can't gulp in enough air. Finally, the official says, "Lacey Johnson tied that goat in twenty-four seconds. Let's have a big round of applause for this cowgirl."

7
8
9

After Lacey unties Gussie's reins, she places her left cowboy boot in the stirrup and swings herself up. Now she needs to ride out of the arena.

Lacey can't remember where the gate is. One of the pickup men rides over with her hat. She doesn't dare ask him where to go. Then as Lacey sets her hat back on, she spots the gate man. *Cowgirl. Cowgirl.* The announcer called her a cowgirl. Lacey feels like riding on forever and ever.